JUN 2 3 '94	**DATE DUE**	
JUL 1 4 '94	JUL 3 0 1998	
JUL 2 1 '94	NOV 1 7 1999	
AUG 1 1 '94	NOV 3 0 1999	
SEP -7 '94	JUL 2 6 2000	
SEP 2 2 '94	NOV 2 2 2000	
NOV 1 7 '94	MAY 1 4 2002	
FEB 9 _ '95	NOV 1 5 2003	
FEB 2 3 '95	NOV 0 4 2004	
MAY 1 1 '95	AUG 2 6 '15	
AUG 2 4 '95	SEP 0 5 '15	
DEC 0 7 '95		

THE TALENT SHOW

· *Louanne Pig in* ·
THE TALENT
SHOW

Nancy Carlson

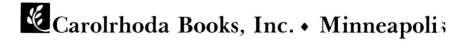

Carolrhoda Books, Inc. · Minneapolis

LIBRARY OF CONGRESS CATALOGING IN PUBLICATION DATA

Carlson, Nancy L.
  Louanne Pig in the talent show.

  Title on added t.p.: The talent show.
  Summary: No-talent Louanne's spirits droop as her
friends prepare for the talent show, but then she is
called upon to perform in a very special way.
  1. Children's stories, American. [1. Performing
arts—Fiction] I. Title.
PZ7.C21665Lkm   1985   [E]   85-4122
ISBN 0-87614-284-6 (lib. bdg.)

  3   4   5   6   7   8   9   10   94   93

To Mrs. Mansfield and Mrs. Blashfield,
two special teachers

Everyone was excited to try out for the annual talent show.

Everyone but Louanne, that is.
"I don't have any talent," she said.

"Why don't you try dancing," suggested Harriet.

"I can't dance," said Louanne.

"How about acrobatics," said Arnie.
"I know I could never do that," said Louanne.

"You could take up the tuba," suggested
George.
"No way!" said Louanne.

"The flute, then," said Tony.
"I can't play *any* instruments," said Louanne.

"I'm going to sing a medley of Broadway tunes," said Ralph. "*Anyone* can sing."

"Not me," said Louanne. "I'm just a big, no-talent dope!"

All week long, everywhere she went,

everyone was practicing.

"Who cares about a dumb old talent show anyway," Louanne muttered.

"I have better things to do."

Tryouts were held on Friday after school.
Harriet made it. Arnie made it. Tony made
it. Ralph made it. Even George made it, but
not as a tuba player.

George was going to be master of ceremonies.
"That's even better," he bragged. "I'll be on
stage ten times more than anyone else!"

"Talent shows are stupid," said Louanne,

and she buried herself in a book.

At last the big night arrived. Louanne thought of all her friends getting ready. She pictured the lights dimming, the curtain slowly rising. She felt miserable.

Suddenly the phone rang. It was Harriet.
She was very upset.

"Louanne, you've just got to help us," she
said. "George has laryngitis!"

"You mean you want *me* to be the master of ceremonies?" asked Louanne.

"George has a wonderful costume," said Harriet. "He says you can wear it. Pleeeease?"

But Louanne wasn't there to answer. She was already on her way to the auditorium.

The evening was a great success.

"Still think talent shows are stupid?" asked
Harriet.

"Who, *me*?" said Louanne.

"I LOVE show biz!"